Bailey Bloom and the Battle of the Bug

JILL ROSENSWEIG

Illustrated by JUDY ELIZABETH WILSON

Zoeicky Press
Los Angeles

This book belongs to

_____

First edition June 2020

Book design by Judy Elizabeth Wilson
Edited by Zelly Zuskin

ISBN 978-1-7352025-1-8 (paperback)

Published by Zoeicky Press

For Jonah and Zoey,
my favorite real-life superheroes,
whose acts of kindness during the Covid-19 pandemic inspired this book.

Deep in the valley,
On a street with bungalows,
Played Bailey Bloom
With Zoey and Rose.

They would run in wide circles,
Games of tag all afternoon,
But when their moms called "dinner!"
They'd take off, saying, "See you soon!"

Each and every morning,
They would reunite in class.
Desks beside each other,
Listening to Ms. Glass.

At lunch, they'd play games
Of the superhero sort.
Each of them had powers;
Bailey chose to teleport.

On Mondays, they'd save a princess.

On Tuesdays, it was a king.

On Wednesdays, they'd stop the bad guys
From stealing a diamond ring.

On Thursdays, they'd stop a fire
From burning down a tower,
While flying on their unicorns
Twinkle, Spark, and Flower.

But Fridays were the best,
When the world was in despair.
The girls would hatch a plan
To save the earth with much fanfare.

The girls loved to imagine
A time when they'd be grown.
They'd be real-life superheroes
With real capes, masks, and a phone.

But late one afternoon,
When Bailey returned from school,
Her mom was in the kitchen
Sitting sadly on a stool.

"I have some news," she started,
"Your school is shutting down.
A bug is going all around
From town to town to town."

"No school?" Bailey pondered.
"But can I see my friends?"
"I'm sad to say the answer's, 'No,'
From now until this ends.

The bug is called Corona,
For kids it's like a cold,
But we need to stay at home
To protect those who are old."

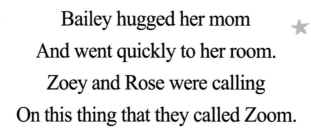

Bailey hugged her mom
And went quickly to her room.
Zoey and Rose were calling
On this thing that they called Zoom.

"Okay, girls, let's do this.
We need to hatch a plan
To stop this thing from spreading
All across the land.

Corona's like a bad guy
Who jumps from person to person.
But if we all just stay at home,
The virus cannot worsen."

"That's right," chimed in Zoey.
"It's quite uncomplicated.
With things like online shopping,
We can all stay isolated!

But some of our older neighbors
Have never shopped from home.
They hardly use computers
And still use a rotary phone."

"Wait, I have an idea!"
Bailey exclaimed with glee.
"What if we deliver things
To elders who are in need?"

The girls together made a list
Of all their older neighbors.
They started making lots of calls
Like good investigators.

And what did they find?
To an alarming degree,
They'd all run out of sugar,
Medicine, and TP!

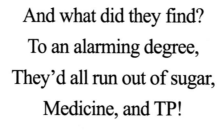

The girls assured their neighbors
They were happy to take orders.
Zoey's brother, Jonah,
Helped drop items at the Border's.

It was all going smoothly,
But something still felt bad.
When people went out walking,
They looked lonely and so sad.

They had to spread some joy
To all those feeling blue.
They'd decorate the streets,
To make things feel brand new.

Zoey put up rainbow art
On every single block.

Rose drew hearts and unicorns
With pastel sidewalk chalk.

Bailey painted river rocks
With bright and smiley faces.
She left them on her neighbors' lawns
To find when running races.

And suddenly others joined
In spreading love around.
Rainbows, hearts, and unicorns
Adorned the entire town.

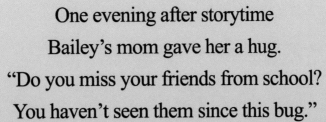

One evening after storytime
Bailey's mom gave her a hug.
"Do you miss your friends from school?
You haven't seen them since this bug."

"I may not see them face-to-face,
And that is sometimes tough.
But teaming up to help others
Somehow feels like it's enough.

I do wish we could be superheroes
Like we always envision.
Get rid of this bug once and for all,
Which is our greatest mission."

Step two was spreading joy
And lowering people's stress,
Which made their bodies stronger
So they could take on any mess!

See, being a real-life superhero
Doesn't require magic powers.
It means you are a helper
During people's hardest hours.

My dear, you are a hero,
As everyone can see.
You fought the virus head-on
And will go down in history."

keep
your
distance

Soon enough it was safe
For the girls to return to class.
Thrilled to be back together,
A feeling nothing could surpass.

When the recess bell rang out,
They would go into the yard.
But their games changed since Corona
In one significant regard.

Of course, they still played superheroes,
But with a very different task.
Now they looked for the kids
Who needed help but were afraid to ask.

Yes, Corona had been hard,
But it taught them something amazing.
You can be a superhero every day
If you look for people who need saving.

Made in the USA
Monee, IL
13 September 2020

42346967R00021